HANDA'S SURPRISE

Read it together

It's never too early to share books with children. Reading together is a wonderful way for your child to enjoy books and stories—and learn to read!

One of the most important ways of helping your child learn to read is by reading aloud—either rereading their favorite books, or getting to know new ones.

Encourage your child to join in with the reading in every possible way. They may be able to talk about the pictures, point to the words, take over parts of the reading, or retell the story afterward.

Can you read it again?

With books they know well, children can try reading to you. Don't worry if the words aren't always the same as th words on the page.

Look, the banana skin! The monkey dropped it.

Will she like the orange?

Will she like the round juicy orange...

If they are reading and get stuck
on a word, show them how to
guess what it says by:
* looking at the pictures
* looking at the letter the word
    begins with
* reading the rest of the sentence
    and coming back to it.
Always help them out if they
get really stuck and or tired.

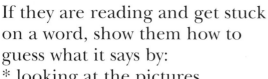

Sometimes you can help children
look more closely at the actual
words and letters. See if they
can find words they recognize,
or letters from their name.
Help write some of the
words they know.

Talk about books with them and
encourage them to discuss stories and
pictures. Compare new books with ones
they already know.

We hope you enjoy reading this book together.

For Emma, Linda, Nadine, and Yewande

The author would like to thank everyone
who helped her research this book,
especially Wanjiru and Nyambura
from the Kenyan Tourist Office,
and Achieng from the Kenyan High Commission.

The children featured in this book
are from the Luo tribe of southwest Kenya.

Copyright © 1994 by Eileen Browne
Introductory and concluding notes copyright © 1998 by CLPE/L B Southwark

Second U.S. edition in this format 1999

Library of Congress Catalog Card Number 98-88069

ISBN 978-0-7636-0863-7

14 15 16 SWT 20 19 18 17

Printed in Dongguan, Guangdong, China

Candlewick Press
99 Dover Street
Somerville, Massachusetts 02144

visit us at www.candlewick.com

HANDA'S SURPRISE

Eileen Browne

CANDLEWICK PRESS

Handa put seven
delicious fruits in a basket
for her friend Akeyo.

She will be surprised,
thought Handa as she set off
for Akeyo's village.

I wonder
which fruit she'll
like best.

Will she like the
soft yellow banana . . .

or the
sweet-smelling guava?

Will she like the
round juicy orange . . .

or the
ripe red mango?

Will she like the
spiky-leaved pineapple . . .

the
creamy green avocado . . .

or the tangy
purple passion fruit?

Which fruit will Akeyo like best?

"Hello, Akeyo," said Handa.
"I've brought you a surprise."

"Tangerines!" said Akeyo.
"My favorite fruit."

"TANGERINES?"
said Handa.
"That *is* a surprise!"

Read it again

monkey

ostrich

zebra

banana

guava

orange

Who took what?
Children can use these pictures to retell the story in their own words.

Story setting
You can discuss with your child where you live and how it is different from Handa's country.

I saw an elephant at the zoo.

Yes, this one's wild.

Words and pictures
Together you can draw pictures of fruits and animals on one set of cards, and then write the names of each one on separate cards. Then match the words to the pictures.

banana

monkey

What's missing?
Starting with ten fruits or other items, children can play a game: Each player takes turns removing one item. The other player has to guess what's missing.

Close your eyes and guess what's missing.

The apple's gone!

Favorite fruits
Make a "fruit book" together, with labeled cutouts or drawings of your child's favorite fruits.

strawberry

apple

grapes

pear

Describing food

In the book, each fruit is described: "soft yellow banana," "round juicy orange." Children can take turns choosing a fruit or vegetable and describing it.

Store

Children can use real or pretend fruit to play "store." With your help, they can make nametags and price tags and they can set up a "counter" with a kitchen scale and a box for toy money.

Read and Share

The Read and Share series is divided into four levels that gradually offer more challenges to new readers. There are stories, poems, songs, traditional tales, and information books to choose from.

Accompanying the series is the *Read and Share Parents' Handbook*, which looks at all the ways children learn to read and explains how *your* help can make a difference!